HOPSCOTCH
TWISTY TALES

Rumpled Stilton Skin

by Daniel Postgate

W
FRANKLIN WATTS
LONDON•SYDNEY

This story is based on the traditional fairy tale,
Rumpelstiltskin, but with a new twist.
You can read the original story in
Hopscotch Fairy Tales. Can you make
up your own twist for the story?

First published in 2012 by
Franklin Watts
338 Euston Road
London
NW1 3BH

Franklin Watts Australia
Level 17/207 Kent Street
Sydney
NSW 2000

Text and illustrations © Daniel Postgate 2012

The rights of Daniel Postgate to be identified as the author
and illustrator of this Work have been asserted
in accordance with the Copyright, Designs and Patents Act, 1988.

A CIP catalogue record for this book is available
from the British Library.

ISBN 978 1 4451 0674 8 (hbk)
ISBN 978 1 4451 0680 9 (pbk)

Series Editor: Melanie Palmer
Series Advisor: Catherine Glavina
Series Designer: Peter Scoulding

Printed in China

Franklin Watts is a division of
Hachette Children's Books,
an Hachette UK company
www.hachette.co.uk

There once lived a young girl
who owned a cheese shop.

She loved to eat all sorts of different cheeses – edam, cheddar, brie … even stilton, which was a very smelly cheese.

But she hated the thick bit of skin
on the end of stilton. It was hard
and rumpled. So she always gave
it to her dog instead. He loved it!

One day, the girl received an
invitation to a royal party.
"I can't go," she moaned.
"All my clothes stink of cheese!"

Just then, a funny man appeared. "I will make you look lovely and smell delightful," he said, "and in return you will give me a present."

"OK," said the girl. So the funny little man set to work. He made her a beautiful dress.

He tidied her hair, and he sprayed
her with the finest perfume.

That evening at the party, the girl looked and smelt terrific.

The King fell in love immediately and asked her to marry him.

11

She said … YES! They were married
at once.

Suddenly, the funny little
man appeared.
"I have come for my present,"
he said.

The King offered him gold,

some land,

and a nice horse,

but the little man refused them all.

"I want your dog," said the man,
licking his lips and rubbing
his tummy.

16

"Oh no!" cried the girl, who was now the Queen. "I love my dog too much to give him to you!"

"Very well," snarled the little man. "I will let you off if you can guess my name in three guesses."

"Fine," said the Queen.

"Is it Bernard?"

"No!" giggled the man. "It's much more unusual than that!"

"OK, is it Toby?"

asked the Queen.

20

"No! No! One more go!" laughed the man, jumping from foot to foot.

The Queen thought the man was nastier than the bit of the cheese she hated so much.

"You are worse than RUMPLED STILTON SKIN!" she cried.

The man stopped dancing and stared at her in disbelief.

"Did you say … Rumpelstiltskin?" he gasped.

"Erm … I think so," said the Queen, fibbing a bit.

"Curses!" exclaimed the man.
"You're right!"

Then he went off in a very bad mood and was never seen again.

And the Queen, her dog and the King (who also liked cheese) lived a very happy and very smelly life together.

Puzzle 1

Put these pictures in the correct order.
Which event do you think is most important?
Now try writing the story in your own words!

Puzzle 2

Choose the correct speech bubbles for each character. Can you think of any others? Turn over to find the answers.

Answers

Puzzle 1

The correct order is: 1e, 2b, 3d, 4f, 5c, 6a

Puzzle 2

The girl/Queen: 1, 4, 6

Rumpelstiltskin: 2, 3, 5

Look out for more Hopscotch Twisty Tales and Fairy Tales:

TWISTY TALES

The Princess and the Frozen Peas
ISBN 978 1 4451 0669 4*
ISBN 978 1 4451 0675 5

Snow White Sees the Light
ISBN 978 1 4451 0670 0*
ISBN 978 1 4451 0676 2

The Elves and the Trendy Shoes
ISBN 978 1 4451 0672 4*
ISBN 978 1 4451 0678 6

The Three Frilly Goats Fluff
ISBN 978 1 4451 0671 7*
ISBN 978 1 4451 0677 9

Princess Frog
ISBN 978 1 4451 0673 1*
ISBN 978 1 4451 0679 3

Rumpled Stilton Skin
ISBN 978 1 4451 0674 8*
ISBN 978 1 4451 0680 9

Jack and the Bean Pie
ISBN 978 1 4451 0182 8

Brownilocks and the Three Bowls of Cornflakes
ISBN 978 1 4451 0183 5

Cinderella's Big Foot
ISBN 978 1 4451 0184 2

Little Bad Riding Hood
ISBN 978 1 4451 0185 9

Sleeping Beauty – 100 Years Later
ISBN 978 1 4451 0186 6

FAIRY TALES

The Three Little Pigs
ISBN 978 0 7496 7905 7

Little Red Riding Hood
ISBN 978 0 7496 7907 1

Goldilocks and the Three Bears
ISBN 978 0 7496 7903 3

Hansel and Gretel
ISBN 978 0 7496 7904 0

Rapunzel
ISBN 978 0 7496 7906 4

Rumpelstiltskin
ISBN 978 0 7496 7908 8

The Elves and the Shoemaker
ISBN 978 0 7496 8543 0

The Ugly Duckling
ISBN 978 0 7496 8544 7

Sleeping Beauty
ISBN 978 0 7496 8545 4

The Frog Prince
ISBN 978 0 7496 8546 1

The Princess and the Pea
ISBN 978 0 7496 8547 8

Dick Whittington
ISBN 978 0 7496 8548 5

Cinderella
ISBN 978 0 7496 7417 5

Snow White and the Seven Dwarfs
ISBN 978 0 7496 7418 2

The Pied Piper of Hamelin
ISBN 978 0 7496 7419 9

Jack and the Beanstalk
ISBN 978 0 7496 7422 9

The Three Billy Goats Gruff
ISBN 978 0 7496 7420 5

For more Hopscotch books go to:

*hardback   www.franklinwatts.co.uk